Written by Fay Robinson
Illustrated By Susan Guevara

■ CelebrationPress

An Imprint of ScottForesman
A Division of HarperCollins*Publishers*

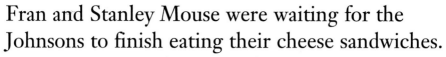

Fran and Stanley Mouse were waiting for the
Johnsons to finish eating their cheese sandwiches.

"Cousin Rita has invited us to visit for the
weekend," Mrs. Johnson said to her husband.

"Well, that sounds like a wonderful idea,"
said Mr. Johnson, as he brushed the crumbs from
his chin.

Fran and Stanley were watching from their
mousehole. "Yes! A wonderful idea!" they
whispered at the same time.

3

The Johnsons finished their lunch, picked up their empty plates, and headed into the kitchen.

Fran and Stanley scurried under the table to clean up the crumbs and scraps.

"Wow! A whole weekend alone! We can have the best party ever!" said Stanley.

"Let's invite everyone we know!" said Fran.

"And tell them to invite everyone THEY know," said Stanley.

Meanwhile, in the kitchen, far away from Fran and Stanley, Mr. Johnson said, "On second thought . . . I don't really feel like going away for the whole weekend."

"Yes, Cousin Rita can be such a bore. Let's just go over for dinner," said Mrs. Johnson.

Their plans were set.

But so were Fran and Stanley's.

5

Fran and Stanley made invitations and hurried out to see their friends.

Mr. and Mrs. Johnson made a bundt cake and hurried out to see Cousin Rita.

Soon Fran and Stanley's guests started arriving. They squeezed in through a crack behind the old sofa.

"Welcome, Belmont, Edith, Bart, Mickey, Minerva, Clementine, . . ." said Fran and Stanley, as their mouse friends trailed in.

6

Stanley showed his guests to the kitchen. "Let's start here," he said, pointing to the refrigerator.

One mouse stood at the base of the refrigerator, and others climbed on his shoulders. The mice stood one on top of the other until they could reach the handle. They yanked the door open and scuttled right to the shelf with the cheese.

"Yummm . . . sliced American . . . cheddar . . . and mozzarella!" they said, as they pushed each package out of the fridge to their friends waiting on the floor.

Soon all the cheese was gone, and the mice were looking around for something to do next.

"I know," said Stanley, "let's make a slide! On the count of three, everyone push the table! One . . . two . . . THREE!"

The kitchen table tipped over and landed at just the right angle. Fran gave each mouse a little piece of butter. The mice spread the butter up and down the table until it was slick and shiny.

"Surf's up!" yelled Stanley, as he slid down on his feet.

Soon all the mice were screeching with delight as they slid down the table every which way.

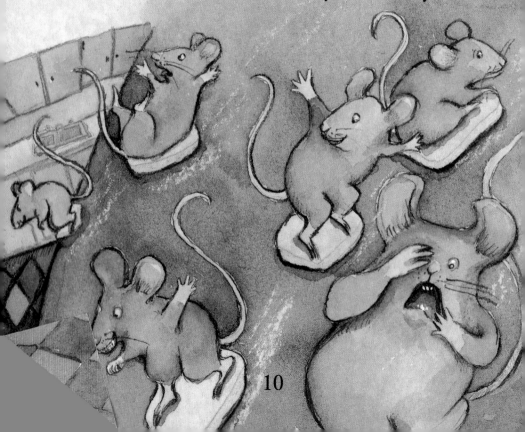

After awhile, the floor was covered with melted butter. The mice were slipping so much they couldn't walk anymore.

"I'm feeling a little greasy," said Stanley, as he stroked his fur. "Follow me if you want to take a shower!"

The mice followed Stanley to the dishwasher. They all jumped in under the jets of warm water. Stanley led his friends in his favorite shower song as they scrubbed under their furry arms and between their furry toes.

"Time to dry off," said Fran. She scampered to the dryer and turned the setting to fluff dry. The mice ran around inside the windy treadmill. "Ahh, the warm air feels like a summer breeze, doesn't it?" asked Fran.

When the dryer came to a stop, all the mice hopped out, all puffy and soft.

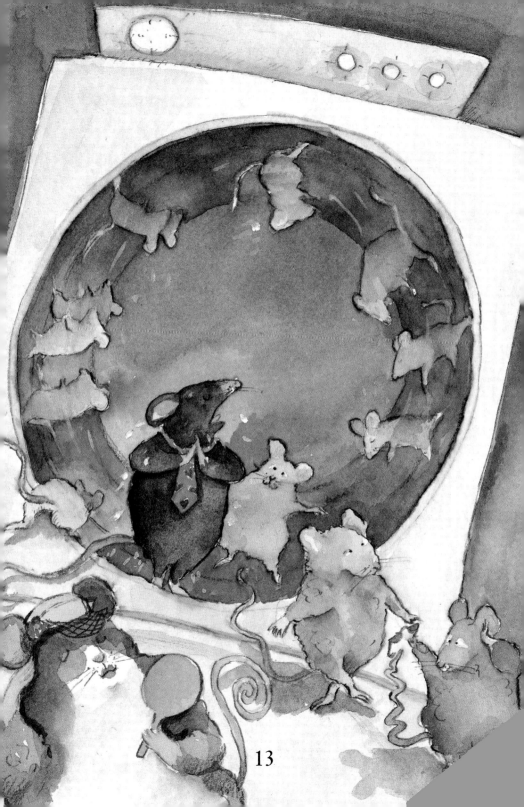

13

"Something's missing," said Stanley. "How about some music?" He dashed to the living room and climbed between the books in the bookcase. Soon he reached the record player. "Let's see," he said. "How does this thing work?"

As Stanley was thinking, some of the mice were playing on the handle. It began to slowly turn. This made the record start to spin.

When the music started, Stanley and the rest of the mice jumped onto the moving record and began to dance. Soon the spinning record was covered with dancing mice. Some held onto the edge of the record with their front paws, letting their feet fly out. Others danced on the long arm that stretched across the record as if it were a bridge.

15

By now every mouse in town knew there was
a big mouse party going on at the Johnsons' house.
Mice were streaming through every hole and crack.
The house was covered with mice.

Most of the mice headed straight for the
kitchen. They dug into the ice cream, using their
tails as spoons. They skated on the floors with ice
cubes strapped to their feet.

In the bedroom, they jumped on the bed, did
flips onto the pillows, and skittered up and down
the bedposts.

They opened all the drawers and ruffled through the Johnsons' clean clothes. Some played hide-and-seek in the socks, while others tunneled through pajama legs. The more stylish mice put on Mrs. Johnson's jewelry, wearing her fancy rings as crowns and her earrings as flashy pins.

In the bathroom, they had diving contests. Some did swan dives off the faucet into the tub, while others rode rubber ducks in the bathwater, bouncing off each other like bumper cars.

The party was getting louder and messier. Music was blaring, the mice were singing and shouting and dancing up a storm, and then . . .

19

the front door opened with a click. But no one
heard it. In walked the Johnsons, happy to be home
from their dinner with their Cousin Rita.

Fran and Stanley were the first to notice them.
"Uh-oh," said Stanley softly.

"What's going on here?" boomed Mr. Johnson.

All the mice stopped dancing and looked up.
Fran turned off the music. Mr. and Mrs. Johnson
looked around the room with wide, startled eyes.

The mice froze, too scared to move. "Looks
like a mouse party," said Mrs. Johnson, winking at
Mr. Johnson.

21

"A mouse party?" asked Mr. Johnson. Then a slow smile crept across his lips.

"Well, what do you know . . . we LOVE parties!" shouted Mr. Johnson.

"Dinner at Cousin Rita's was OK, but THIS is my idea of a fun Saturday night!" agreed Mrs. Johnson.

The Johnsons danced with the mice until they wore holes in their socks.

And then they danced and danced some more!